MARGARET BARBALET

THE WOLF

illustrated by

JANE TANNER

Macmillan Publishing Company New York
Maxwell Macmillan Canada Toronto
Maxwell Macmillan International Publishing Group
New York   Oxford   Singapore   Sydney

The first time Tal heard the wolf he didn't believe it. He went back to sleep. The next time it woke all of them. But after a while they fell asleep again.

Next morning in the kitchen, however, things were not the same. Around the breakfast table they began to discuss wolves.

'They don't live *here*, in this part of the country,' their mother said firmly.

'Where *do* they live?' Dai, the youngest, asked.

Tal and Megan looked at each other. Mother didn't answer. Then it was time to go to school and they forgot about Dai's question.

That night Tal heard the wolf in their
own garden.

Next morning before their mother was even awake,
Tal got out the encyclopedia.

'We live in open peaceful country. We always have.'
Megan was close to tears. 'They can't come here.'

Together they looked at the colored pictures.
There was a wolf eating a bloodied mess, red leaking
into the snow. Tal shut the book. They knew Dai
must never see it.

That night Tal was unable to go to sleep.

He thought of the hill that sheltered their house, the trees and rocks they had always played around. They knew every tree and every rock. They always walked to school. Their friends came over to play. As he went to sleep Tal thought, *I think of it always as sunlit, peaceful. I know it rains, but I think of it as a peaceful place.*

He awoke to Dai's scream, to the house shaking as their mother ran downstairs to lock the windows.

The howling went on and on. He knew it was the wolf coming closer. It was worse than he could have imagined. It was worse than his nightmares.

It was the worst thing, coming closer every night.

The next day, without even mentioning wolves, their mother outlined some of the new rules.

They would have to always play inside. The doors would have to be bolted and barred. Here mother looked at Tal. He was sometimes careless.

'What about school?' Dai asked.

Their mother frowned. 'I'll have to take you in the car.'

'Every day?' Megan asked, then stopped. 'Of course it'll be every day. I wasn't thinking.'

That night their mother went around the house bolting shut all the windows. Some of them had never been bolted before, and stuck. She had to force and wedge them shut. It took a long time and it was dark by the time she had finished.

'I'm covered in lumps,' announced Dai at breakfast.
He pulled up his pajama jacket. His chest and
stomach were bright red.

'They weren't there yesterday,' mother decided.
'Let's see if they go by tomorrow.'

She packed the bag to take out to the car.
In the new routine they all followed her and
jumped in as she slammed the front door shut.

I just wish she'd say something, anything. . .
Tal thought as they drove off to school.
She didn't talk about the wolf;
but everything had
changed.

Next day Dai's lumps had grown together.

'It might be something he ate,' mother pretended, rubbing in the cream they used for mosquito bites.

It might be the wolf, Tal thought silently, *just the idea of it*.

That night Tal awoke aware that Dai had been crying for some time. Megan stood helplessly by his bed. Mother came downstairs from her bedroom.

'What's the matter? Have you had a dream?'

'No, I'm crying because the wolf's come. Because it used to be safe and now it's not.'

Tal heard his mother kiss Dai and tuck him in her own bed. Later he heard crying again.

In secret at school Tal read all about families who had lived surrounded by wolves. He looked at the snow and tundra where the wolves prowled. At home their garden was turning into a wilderness.

At night now they ate dinner trying to talk of other things, arguing the way they had before the wolf came. Mother often turned on the radio so that there would be a cheerful background noise. After a few weeks Tal noticed that she always hummed the same tune, a new one that went down and down.

In bed he would hear the howling coming closer and
closer, leaping over the garden wall. Then he would
hear the wolf prowling around the house, testing every
doorknob, pressing every
window latch. Some nights he
lay rigid with fear so that he had
to turn on his bedside light.
He would fall asleep with it on.

In the kitchen one weekend when Megan and Dai were watching television, he asked about his cat.

'What if I let it out?'

His mother turned, horrified, her hands covered in flour.

'I mean, would that satisfy the wolf? Would it go away?'

'Oh, love,' she said hugging him. 'Of course it wouldn't.'

'What if I went out?' he said beginning to cry. 'It would be worth it for Megan and Dai. Dai's little.'

She hugged him again. 'Tal, I know what you mean. But you can't make it go away.'

'Can anyone?'

'No.'

egan had been the loudest girl he had ever known. Now she was so busy that she didn't have time to shout.

'I want to make it like before the wolf came. I think about that every day,' she said brushing her teeth that night.

'But you can't,' Tal said kindly.

'Well, I will,' she shouted and rushed into her own room.

Later through the wall he heard her beginning to hum. It was the same final tune that his mother always sang.

Months passed. They stopped talking about the wolf. It came every night and they were no longer shocked. Tal had his birthday and asked a few friends. He played his records very loud and after they had all left he realized that no one had even mentioned the wolf.

'You know, I don't think it's as loud as it used to be any more,' he said. 'And from the front this just looks like a normal house.'

His mother looked at him startled, then interested.

That night he sat in his room surrounded
by all his new presents (more than usual, he
guessed, to make up for the wolf). He thought of the
time before the wolf came, and saw it as distant, green
and sunlit, his family in a dream that he could never
go back to. It was like being younger, he thought; that
too was dear to him. And yet he couldn't ever have it
back again. In the flames of the candles on his cake
he had seen himself, unable to go back ever
to the last year.

A week after his birthday when they were washing up his mother said out of a long silence, 'You know, I think you're right. It's definitely a lot softer than it used to be.'

'But still close,' he began. 'You know, Mom, there's a boy at school whose family lived surrounded by wolves for a whole year!'

'What did they do?'

'The same as us. Boarded up their windows, stayed inside all the time.'

'And now?'

'It was in a different part of the country, Mom, not *here*.'

Tal noticed next that while the wolf still prowled around every night it often whined and growled instead of howling. Once Tal went to the window at night in the silences between its howls. He could hear it outside, scratching and panting. He imagined its tongue bobbing on an open jaw among the row of teeth. He put his face up to the boards one night but all he could see was a crack of night sky.

Half a year passed. Megan had her birthday. Dai adapted to life inside, inventing new games for them all on the stairs. Tal supposed they might never go outside in the garden again.

Then towards the end of the year, his mother put down her papers as he came in to say goodnight. It was something from work as usual.

'I'd like you not to tell the others this, Tal, but I've seen the wolf. I took down a board from a high up window.'

As Tal stared she said, 'He's not as big as I thought.'

A week later Tal had a dream. A voice came out of the night: he couldn't tell from where. And the voice spoke and said one thing over and over again: *Let it in, let it in.* Only when he woke up did he realize that the voice was his own.

Tal crept downstairs before it was light to bake Mom's cake on the morning of her birthday. He always did this. When the cake was in the oven he made himself some breakfast.

Suddenly he heard a rasping. Something was snoring right outside the kitchen door. Suddenly he had to see.

He went and found a strong kitchen knife and pried off one end of a board. It cracked as he took it away. Sunlight flooded his face; as startling as the sight of the wolf, awakened by the sound, bounding away in fright over their garden wall.

When his mother saw the missing board she smiled. Tal was so relieved that he found himself telling her about his dream and the voice saying, *Let it in, let it in*.

'I've had the same dream lately,' she said.

That night he had the dream again. He awoke in the dark still hearing the voice. In his pajamas he went down the stairs. He could hear the wolf outside the door, whining. Suddenly he realized that it was almost morning, half light. He wanted more than anything to go outside.

Let it in, let it in, said the voice at his elbow.

With a reckless movement he took down the bar, cobwebbed and dirty, and opened the lock on the door. Then he pulled open the door, wide, and stood back.

There stood the wolf, dirty and thin. Its hair was matted and grey. It looked at him and then limped past into the living room and lay down in front of the dying fire's warmth. It left muddy footprints and its tail knocked down a magazine.

It's like a dog, he thought.

Outside the garden waited, green
and wonderful, just touched with the
color of sunrise.

Tal went and woke the others and led them, holding
Dai's hand, down to the living room.

  'I've let the wolf in,' he said proudly. He smiled.
'I think it might stay with us.'

For Ann Jungman – M.B.
For those who have the courage to keep looking – J.T.

Text copyright © 1992 by Margaret Barbalet

Illustrations copyright © 1992 by Jane Tanner

Macmillan Publishing Company is part of the Maxwell Communication
Group of Companies.

Macmillan Publishing Company
866 Third Avenue
New York, NY 10022

Maxwell Macmillan Canada, Inc.
1200 Eglinton Avenue East
Suite 200
Don Mills, Ontario M3C 3N1

First American edition

Printed in Hong Kong by Bookbuilders Ltd.

10 9 8 7 6 5 4 3 2 1

The text of this book is set in Caslon
The illustrations are rendered in pencil, water colour and gouache

Library of Congress CIP data is available.
ISBN 0-02-711840-1